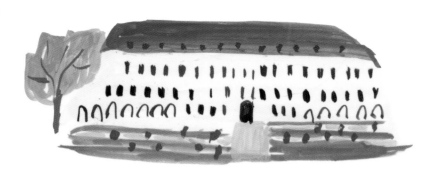

JEANNE MOREAU

OTHER BOOKS IN THE SERIES

Paris-Chien: Adventures of an Expat Dog

Hudson in Provence

For Steve.

Special thanks to Jil, Lynn, Robin, Sarah and Stephen.

Library of Congress Cataloging-in-Publication Data

Names: Mancuso, Jackie Clark, author, illustrator.
Title: Hudson and the puppy : lost in Paris / by Jackie Clark Mancuso.
Description: Los Angeles. CA : La Librairie Parisienne, [2018] | Series: A
   Paris-chien adventure | Summary: Hudson, an American dog living in Paris,
   takes a lost puppy on a whirlwind tour of the city, hoping the pup will
   recognize his neighborhood.
Identifiers: LCCN 2017037231 | ISBN 9780988605855 (hardback)
Subjects: | CYAC: Dogs--Fiction. | Paris (France)--Fiction. |
   France--Fiction. | BISAC: JUVENILE FICTION / Animals / Dogs. | JUVENILE
   FICTION / People & Places / Europe.
Classification: LCC PZ7.M312179 Hr 2018 | DDC [E]--dc23
LC record available at https://lccn.loc.gov/2017037231

ISBN 978-0-9886058-5-5

10 9 8 7 6 5 4 3 2 1

A PARIS-CHIEN ADVENTURE

HUDSON and the PUPPY

LOST IN PARIS

Jackie Clark Mancuso

LA LIBRAIRIE PARISIENNE

BOULANGERIE PÂT

Hi. My name is Hudson.
I live in Paris.
Every morning I go to
the *boulangerie* for a
warm *baguette*.

A few times a week I go to the *cinéma*.
I love watching movies. Especially movies
with dogs!

CINEMA LA PAGODE

Then I take the *métro* to *Jardin des Plantes*. It's a beautiful garden with a zoo and a merry-go-round.

THIS WORKER IS REMOVING OLD ADVERTISING POSTERS

I have
a feeling
I'm being
followed.

DODO MANÈGE, JARDIN DES PLANTES

"Are you lost? Would you like me to help you? Can you talk?"

Maybe he's shy, or scared.

I think he's just a puppy. Maybe he doesn't know how to talk yet.

"I know Paris pretty well.
I can help you find your way home.
Let's look for a neighborhood you recognize.
I just have to be home by dinnertime."

"We'll start here
in my favorite park.
This man makes delicious
crêpes. Have you seen
him before?"

LE KIOSQUE A CREPES, JARDIN DU LUXEMBOURG

We cross the
River Seine to
Montmartre.

This neighborhood
has lots of dogs.

"Have you ever
climbed these stairs?"

ESCALIER DE LA RUE FOYATIER,
MONTMARTRE

We can use a scooter to get around more quickly.
Paris is a big city.

"This neighborhood has food from all over the world. Curry, kebabs, and Turkish pizza."

"Does it smell familiar?"

DOME DES INVALIDES
TOMBEAU DE NAPOLEON

TOUR EIFFEL

"Let's try one more thing."
We hop on a boat that takes us
from one end of Paris to the other.
In the middle of the ride, I have a scary thought.

Maybe he doesn't
have a home.

Maybe he never had a home.

"Don't worry, puppy If you don't have a home, we can find you one. Someone will want to adopt you."

We waited a very long time.

CHIOT gRATUiT!
caractère «impeccable»

FREE PUPPY "sterling" character

But no one wanted
my new friend.

"I'm allergic."
"J'ai des allergies."

"I have a cat."
"J'ai un chat."

"I'm never home."
"Je ne suis jamais
chez moi."

"He's too big."
"Il est trop grand."

"He's too small."
"Il est trop petit."

GRAND ACTION CINÉMA,
RUE DES ECOLES,
QUARTIER LATIN

UN FILM DE
JACQUES
TATI

We were feeling blue.

"Good idea,
puppy!
A movie will
cheer us up.
There's just
enough time
before I have
to be home."

Seeing the movie
together gave me
a new idea.

"Wait here!
Ne bouge pas!"

"I asked my mom. If you like, this can be your home too. It would make me very happy."

"*Ça va?*
Would you like that?"

"*Wouaf!*
Ça va!"

Maybe that's what he wanted all along.
I named him Pierre and now we eat *baguettes*,
ride the carousel, and see lots of movies, together.

le petit dictionnaire

boulangerie [boo-lawn-jree] .... bakery

patisserie [pah-tiss-ree] .... pastry shop

cinéma [sin-eh-muh] .... movie theater

cinéphile [sin-eh-feel] .... film lover

métro [meh-trow] .... subway

bonjour [bon-juhr] .... hello

manège [mah-nej] .... carousel

ménagerie [meh-naj-ree] .... zoo

crêpes [crehp] .... pancakes

fromage [froh-maj] .... cheese

escalier [es-cahl-yay] .... stairs

chiot [she-oh] .... puppy

gratuit [grah-twee] .... free

caractère [car-ac-tair] .... character

impeccable [am-peh-kabl] .... impeccable

Le Gosse [luh gos] .... The Kid

ne bouge pas [nuh booj pa] .... don't move

collier [cull-yay] .... collar

poulpe [poolp] .... octopus

éléphant [eh-lay-fon] .... elephant

feu d'artifice [fuh dar-tee-fiece] .... fireworks

Ça va? [sah vah] .... OK?

Ça va. [sah vah] .... OK.

"Le film commence quand le spectateur sort de la salle."—François Truffaut